WAX

Please renew or return items by the date shown on your receipt

www.hertfordshire.gov.uk/libraries

Renewals and enquiries: 0300 123 4049

Textphone for hearing or 0300 123 4041
speech impaired users:

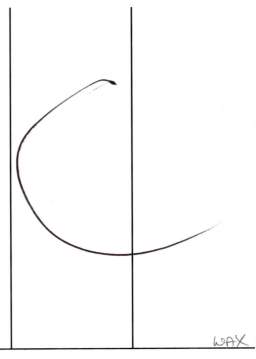

L32 11.16

526 809

First published in Great Britain by Scribo MMXVIII
Scribo, an imprint of
The Salariya Book Company
25 Marlborough Place, Brighton, BN1 1UB

ISBN 978-1-912233-20-5

Book design by David Salariya

Printed and bound in China

The text for this book is set in Century Schoolbook
The display type is Jacob Riley

www.salariya.com

Illustrations: Sarah Horne

THE LONG-LOST SECRET DIARY OF THE WORLD'S WORST ASTRONAUT

Written by
Tim Collins

Illustrated by
Sarah Horne

SCRIBO
a SALARIYA *imprint*

GET REAL

Unlike the other books in this series, this diary is set in the near future rather than the distant past. But right now, it wouldn't be possible for someone as young as Ellie to become an astronaut. NASA only considers candidates with a degree in science subjects or engineering, as well as three years of professional experience. They are also often experienced pilots and incredibly fit.

Chapter I

Accidental Astronaut

Monday June 29th

Mars, here we come. Not me personally. By 'we'
I mean us humans. The first mission to the red
planet is almost ready.

Today we stood on the viewing platform in
the Space Centre here in Florida and watched
a rocket filled with supplies take off for the
Mars ship.

Dad works in the finance department, so he's allowed to bring us along.

The countdown boomed out through the speakers.

'T minus one minute... T minus 30 seconds... 10... 9... 8... 7... 6... 5... 4... 3... 2... 1...'

The engines fired up and the rocket shot away in a bright flash of orange. The smell of burning fuel mixed in with the distant smell of the ocean.

Soon the three best astronauts in the world are going to fly up to the Mars ship, which is currently orbiting the Earth. They're going to travel to Mars, build a lab, carry out some experiments and come back.

I wish I was one of them. I wish it so hard. Dad always said I'd be old enough to be an astronaut by the time a Mars mission happened. But things have happened so fast in the last few years, faster than anyone expected.

Ten of the world's nations came together and funded the project. Now we're less than three months from take-off, and five months from the first human footprint on Mars.

Or boot print, rather. If I were them I'd keep my shoes on.

The rocket disappeared through the clouds, leaving a thick column of smoke. The announcer thanked us for coming and we filed away.

Mom asked if I was okay while we were driving home. I told her I was fine. How could I explain I was upset because I couldn't go to Mars? I'd have sounded crazy.

GET REAL

The first challenge of a human mission to Mars would be leaving Earth. It would be very hard to build a rocket big enough to carry crew and supplies that was also powerful enough to escape Earth's gravitational pull. A good solution would be to build the ship in the orbit of Earth and send the astronauts up when it was complete.

Tuesday June 30th

I'm going back to the Space Centre tomorrow. But not to watch another launch. School is out for summer, and I convinced Dad to let me study in the library next to his office.

I don't really have much work to do. I just want to be near the rockets. I might even sneak into one of the hangars on the edge of the centre

and look at one. I'll keep that bit quiet from
Dad, though. He'd never let me come along if he
knew I was planning something like that.

Wednesday July 1ˢᵗ

I'm writing this from the Space Centre library.
I took a stroll outside at lunchtime but every
building had guards around it. I can see why
they need to keep security tight with the Mars
mission so close, but they've got to take a break
at some point. I really want to see a rocket.

Thursday July 2ⁿᵈ

I was heading over to the lunch hall today
when I saw that a lot of the security guards
were gone. At first I was worried they might be
dealing with some sort of intruder, but I soon
saw a huge crowd and worked out what was
going on.

There was a TV crew walking around and interviewing people. The guards and most of the other workers were huddled around them, waiting for their chance to speak.

The row of hangars with the rocket parts inside were a few hundred metres away, on Venus Boulevard. I made a run for the nearest one.

The fierce midday heat sent sweat trickling down my back, but I didn't care. I was really close now. The first hangar I came to had an empty security booth next to its wide entrance, and I rushed in.

I found myself in a dark, stuffy space that smelled of fresh paint. There was no air conditioning and the strip lights far above me were off. But I could see something pretty awesome right ahead.

There was a huge circular section of rocket, surrounded by ladders and scaffolding. I stepped up and placed my hand on it. Just touching it made me feel a little closer to the Mars mission. I told myself I'd remember this moment when I watched the astronauts touching down.

'Hey,' came a voice from the doorway. 'What are you doing in there?'

I spun round. I could see the outline of a man against the bright light.

One of the guards, I guessed. I tried to work out what to say. If I admitted I'd been sneaking around, Dad could get in trouble.

'I'm an astronaut,' I said. 'They sent me here to check on this new rocket and I think it's just fine.' I turned around and tapped it. 'Yeah. Pretty good rocket.'

'You don't seem old enough to be an astronaut,' said the man.

'I'm the youngest there's ever been,' I said. 'They chose me for their training scheme to get teenagers interested in space stuff.'

That was actually a pretty good lie. Much better than my usual. But had the man bought it? I couldn't see his face.

'We need to get this!' he shouted, beckoning someone else over.

Soon the bright doorway was filled with people.

There was a click and the lights blinked on.

Now I could see the man clearly. He was wearing a clean white shirt and carrying a tablet. Next to him was a woman with a clipboard, a guy holding a huge furry microphone and a guy carrying a camera. In front of them, marching towards me was a woman in a red dress. I recognised her as Martha Sanchez from the evening news.

'That's her,' said the man in the white shirt. 'She's going to be the youngest astronaut in history.'

'Good angle,' said Martha. 'Why didn't they tell us about this?'

Uh-oh.

A small voice in my head told me this was not a great idea. That it would be better for me to run away than repeat my lie for millions of TV viewers. But it was too late to back out.

A minute later the boom mic was floating over my head and the camera was pointing at my face.

'So how did you get selected for this mission?' asked Martha.

'They sent special space talent scouts out to every school,' I said. 'Then they made a shortlist of a hundred people and I was chosen.'

I was getting into it now. I'd almost forgotten it was a lie.

'And what kind of training have they given you?' asked Martha.

'Zero gravity training,' I said, searching

my mind for other words that would sound plausible. 'And general space stuff.'

Ouch. I didn't pull that off very well.

'And what is it that makes Mars so special?' asked Martha.

Now this I could answer. I love space travel and the Mars trip is the most exciting thing that's happened in my life.

'Humans have always been curious,' I said. 'We've wanted to make that next step, whether it's across the ocean or into the stars. We got to the Moon over fifty years ago. Now it's time to go further.'

Martha slapped her hand down on my shoulder. 'I'm sure all of America will be rooting for you.'

She turned to her camera man and made a circle with her thumb and forefinger. They stopped filming.

I looked behind her and saw a security guard striding towards us. My heart sank. After all the effort I'd put into my interview, he was going to reveal I was faking.

18

I shrank back as he approached. But when
he reached us he just tapped Martha on the
shoulder and said, 'Hey, interview me next. I'll
tell you about the time some eagles nested in
that roof.'

Update
Okay, I think I got away with it.

I got worried that Dad would see the news
bulletin and know I'd been sneaking around. So
I distracted him with a tough math problem.
He was confused about why I was studying so
hard on summer break. But he can never resist
helping me with school stuff, so it worked fine.
It kept him busy the whole time the evening
news was on, and now he'll never know what
I did.

Friday July 3rd

Dad pulled into his regular parking spot this morning and made his way towards the door of his building. One of the security guards rushed out and said, 'Bradley Anderson needs to see you urgently.'

Dad went pale. Bradley Anderson is the head of IASA, the International Aeronautics and Space Administration, the organisation that runs the Space Centre and all the missions. He's Dad's boss. Not just his immediate boss, but the guy way at the top.

'Hope things are okay,' I said, heading over to the library.

'You too,' said the security guard, pointing at me.

I froze in the middle of a stride. This was not good.

If Bradley wanted to see me too, he must have found out I'd been sneaking around. What if Dad got fired? Trespassing is really serious.

We followed the guard through the wide, clean lobby and into the elevator.

There was a panel of buttons next to the door. The guard pressed the top one and we swooshed up.

Dad folded his arms and peered at me. 'Any idea why Bradley wants to see you too?'

'I might have accidentally left the library yesterday,' I said. 'My pen ran out and I went to look for a new one and I think I might have ended up in one of the hangars next to a rocket.'

Dad turned bright red. 'Right, because that's where you get pens from, isn't it? The rocket hangars.'

He was scrunching his fists into tight balls and the veins in his temples were bulging. 'I should have known something like this would happen.'

'I'm not grounded, am I?' I asked.

He said nothing. That meant he was really angry.

The doors pinged open and the guard led us into a large office. To our left was a window that looked out to the launch site in the far distance, and the ocean beyond it.

Bradley Anderson was sitting behind a desk. He was wearing a shirt with an IASA patch sewn on the pocket.

'Take a seat,' he said.

I grabbed one of the chairs in front of him. There was a plastic model of the Mars ship on his desk and I had to sit on my hands to stop myself grabbing it. It was a cool model. They'd even included the huge wheel that spins around the middle section.

'If this is about my daughter wandering around the site, I can explain,' said Dad.

Bradley Anderson just stared at him and pointed to the free chair. Dad slouched down into it and folded his arms.

Bradley tapped a button on his laptop and turned it round to face us. I felt my heart sink. He had a clip of Martha's news report cued up. After all my attempts to keep it secret, Dad was going to see it after all.

'I may have accidentally spoken to some TV people too yesterday,' I said. 'I forgot to mention that.'

We watched my interview. The words 'Mars Girl' stayed on the bottom of the screen the whole time.

When it ended, Bradley turned his computer back around.

'That report was broadcast just after seven last night,' he said. He peered at his screen. 'Since then it has been viewed over three million times. I've had over a thousand emails from media outlets wanting to know more about Mars Girl. And I've just been informed that the president himself has retweeted it.'

My mind was racing. I was famous. Everyone in the world would know me as Mars Girl, and I could sign autographs and pose for selfies and...

Except that I wasn't really Mars Girl, was I?

I was Liar Girl. That's how they'd all know me when the facts got out.

'It seems to me that there's only one course of action open to us...' said Bradley.

'We're very sorry about what has happened,' said Dad. 'I assure you nothing like this will happen again if you just...'

Bradley held his hands up. 'I don't think you understand me,' he said. 'I'm not trying to punish you. I'm suggesting we enrol your daughter in our training program, starting right away.'

I had to play Bradley's words back in my mind to make sure I'd understood them. Was he really saying I could be an astronaut?

This time I couldn't stop myself. I grabbed the

toy ship from Bradley's desk and made it fly through the air.

I was actually going to Mars. This was the best thing that had ever happened to me.

Dad leaned forward and clenched his hands together.

'You can't send her up there,' he said. 'It's way too dangerous. Your astronauts understand the risks they're taking. She doesn't. She's just a child.'

'Hey,' I said. 'I'll be driving next year. You need to drop the 'just a child' stuff if you want me to pick you up from bowling.'

'I don't mean we'll actually select her,' said Bradley.

Oh. So much for the Mars trip, then. I put the plastic rocket back on the desk.

'But she'll go through all the training with the real astronauts,' said Bradley. 'And she can give reports on TV and YouTube and whatnot.

There are still a great many taxpayers who think this Mars trip is a big waste of their cash. But I think Ellie here can win them over. They already love her, based on the comments on the news report. Except for a man calling himself AstroTroll1994, but you can't please them all.'

'Okay,' said Dad. He turned to me. 'What do you think, Ellie?'

The last few minutes had been hard to take in. First I thought I'd got Dad fired and I'd feel guilty for the rest of my life. Then for one awesome second I thought I was actually going to Mars. Now I'd found out I wasn't going after all, but I could still train as an astronaut.

'Of course I'll do it,' I said.

Bradley stood up and held his hand out. I bolted up and shook it.

'Welcome to the team,' he said.

Saturday July 4th

Fireworks in the park tonight. I got recognised by a whole bunch of people who'd watched the news report and wanted selfies. I didn't even get to see that many of the fireworks this year. I feel a little fake for getting all this attention when I'm not really an astronaut yet. But from Monday I'm going to train hard, and soon I'll become Mars Girl for real.

Chapter 2

—

Meeting the Trainees

Sunday July 5th

I prepared today by reading a book called '101 Wow Facts about Mars'. There were some pretty good things in there. Mars is about half the size of Earth and has similar stuff like valleys and volcanoes, but much better ones. The biggest volcano is more than twice as tall as anything we've got. And it has a canyon that's four times deeper than the Grand Canyon.

I remember how much my mind was blown when we went to the Grand Canyon two summers ago. Imagine what it must be like to stare at something four times as deep.

I'm going to be so jealous of the astronauts who get picked. But at least I'll know them, and have trained with them.

Every day on Mars is 40 minutes longer, which sounds kind of useful, especially if you're allowed to add them to your lunch break.

Years last longer on Mars too, and not just because all those extra minutes add up. It takes longer to go round the Sun, so every year is 687 days long. If I were there now I'd be just eight years old. Which is the exact age Mom treats me anyway.

Mars is also much colder than Earth, with an average temperature of minus 81 degrees Fahrenheit*. This is partly because it's further away from the Sun and partly because it doesn't have the right sort of atmosphere to keep heat in.

As well as the cold temperatures, it has huge dust storms that cover the entire planet. It sounds like a tough place to be. But I'd still go right now if they asked me.

*This is minus 62.7 degrees Celsius.

GET REAL

Each day on Mars lasts for about 40 minutes longer than an Earth day. This is because it takes longer to rotate on its axis. Things are very different elsewhere in our solar system, however. A day on Venus lasts 5,832 hours, while a day on Jupiter lasts just ten hours.

Monday July 6th

I had to report to a lecture theatre on Jupiter Boulevard in the north of the Space Centre this morning. It was like one of the classrooms in my school except with comfortable padded chairs instead of broken plastic ones.

There was a man wearing a green shirt standing at the front. He was projecting a diagram of Mars onto a large screen. On the seats were ten astronaut trainees.

35

'Hi, Ellie,' he said. 'Take a seat. I'm Professor Mike Conrad and I teach orbital mechanics.'

I slunk into the nearest chair on the front row.

'Everyone, this is Ellie Hill, our newest trainee. Be nice to her, because she'll play an important role in winning over the hearts and minds of the public.'

I whipped my head round and waved at the others. It was weird knowing that three of them would go to Mars. I was sitting with the three most famous people I'd ever meet, only I didn't know which ones they were yet.

One by one, the others introduced themselves. They were:

Emma, from the USA

Dev, from India

Li, from China

Dmitry, from Russia

Hana, from Japan

Fabian, from Germany

Jack, from the UK

Emily, from Canada

Aurélie, from France

Matheus, from Brazil

There's one astronaut from every country funding the Mars Mission. Or at least there was. There's two from the USA now I'm on the team.

Professor Conrad turned back to me. 'I'm going to continue as normal,' he said. 'If you have trouble keeping up, raise your hand and I'll try and fill you in.'

'Don't worry,' said Jack. 'It's not rocket science. Oh wait, yes it is.'

There were groans from the others.

'Someone always has to make that joke,' said Emma.

Professor Conrad projected a series of diagrams. I thought I could follow what he was saying. Sort of.

I glanced over my shoulder to see how the others were enjoying it. They were all totally engrossed, making notes in their books and staring at the diagrams with their pens in their mouths. I was pretty surprised, because they looked kind of sporty, and most people like that in my school hate science and math.

I turned back to the screen. There were drawings of circles and curves around rockets and planets that I think were meant to show orbits or flight paths or something. Professor Conrad had told me to stick my hand up and ask if there was a bit I didn't understand, but every time I played something back in my head to check if I'd got it or not, he'd moved on.

At the end of the lecture, he asked me if I'd kept up okay. I didn't want to admit that I hadn't, so I hit him with some hot Mars facts.

'Every day on Mars has an extra 40 minutes,' I said. 'And every year is 687 days long. And the average temperature is minus 81 degrees Fahrenheit.'

Professor Conrad stared at me for a moment, wincing a little. Then he reached into his bag and pulled out a piece of paper.

'Okay,' he said, handing it over. 'Here's a reading list. You might find the ones near the top easier.'

I scanned down the list. The books were called things like 'Advanced Astrodynamics'. They all looked a lot tougher than '101 Wow Facts about Mars'.

Tuesday July 7th

I was told to report to the training facility
on Saturn Boulevard today, so I ate a large
breakfast of pancakes with syrup to make sure
I had a lot of energy.

The facility turned out to be a huge grey
warehouse with the IASA logo on the side. The
automatic doors swished aside as I approached,
letting out a warm, clean smell.

Inside was a small lobby leading to a long
corridor. I spotted Dev, and I jogged after him.

'Any idea where we're meant to go?' I asked.

'I'm going in there,' he said, pointing to a
door at the end of the corridor with a male
symbol on it. 'But you should go that way.'
He pointed to a door opposite with a female
symbol on. 'Your suit should be inside.'

'Cool,' I said. 'Thanks.'

This sounded good. After just one day of stuffy lessons, I was going to get into a spacesuit. It was time to become a proper astronaut.

I pushed the door open. Inside was a changing room with rows of lockers lining each wall and two wooden benches in the middle. The locker nearest to the door was open. I looked inside and saw a space suit waiting for me.

Now I recognised the smell. It was a swimming pool. So after my math lesson I was getting a swimming lesson? What did that have to do with Mars? Who wants to swim when it's minus 81 degrees Fahrenheit anyway?

I pulled my suit on and wandered to the far end of the changing room, where a sign pointed to something called the 'Neutral Buoyancy Lab'.

Okay, so maybe it wasn't a pool, then, but it certainly smelled like one.

I followed a corridor to a huge indoor space. I was right the first time. There was a pool. The biggest one I'd ever seen, in fact. It was the size of a football field and so deep that a section of the Mars ship had been built in it. The revolving circular part reached all the way from the bottom to the surface of the water.

The pool was surrounded by high walls with the flags of all the IASA countries draped over them. It looked like some weird new Olympic event was going to happen.

Most of the other trainees were lining the far side of the pool. But Li was on top of a raised platform to my left, pulling himself into a heavy spacesuit. Dev emerged from the male changing room and clambered up next to him.

A woman with red hair ran over to me holding an oxygen pack.

'Hi,' she said. 'I'm Mia. I'm one of the support divers here at the Neutral Buoyancy Lab. Any questions before we begin?'

I had quite a few, so it was hard to know which one to start with.

'Yes,' I said. 'Why am I standing in front of a huge swimming pool with a spaceship in it?'

'Oh, okay,' said Mia. 'I thought they would have taken you through this, but that's fine. When you're underwater you get a floating feeling that's similar to weightlessness. So you can use the pool to prepare for moving around in space.'

She fixed the oxygen pack to my back.

44

'You've been diving before, right?' she asked.

'Sure,' I said. It was kind of true. We went on holiday to Barbados a few years back and I went on a diving trip with Mom and Dad. But as soon as I got below the surface I thought I saw a shark so I stayed right next to the boat the whole time.

'We'll start the exercise as soon as Dev and Li are in their suits,' she said. 'They're going to practise replacing a panel outside the crew quarters. The rest of you will go down to observe. They'll still be a while getting ready so if you want to dive in and get used to the water, go ahead.'

'Okay,' I said.

I swam a few feet down and looked at the ship through the clear water. The replica of the circular section was spinning slowly around the main ship. It must have cost so much money to build.

I drew level with the wheel and swam next to it as it rotated around the replica. I traced the huge circle in the water, imagining I was floating in space with blue Earth behind me and red Mars ahead of me.

It was then that I realised something very important – I shouldn't have eaten so many pancakes for breakfast.

I padded up to the surface and hoped the world would stop spinning. It didn't.

'What's wrong?' asked Mia. 'You look green.'

I opened my mouth to reply and was horrified to see a huge jet of vomit arcing out of my

mouth and splatting across the surface of
the pool.

All the other astronauts turned to look at me.

'Sorry,' I said. 'I shouldn't have eaten all
those pancakes.'

'Okay,' shouted Mia. 'Hold off on the exercise.
We need to get that barf out of the pool.'

Over on the platform, Dev and Li were in their
space suits, ready to start. They sat down,
folded their arms and glared at me.

GET REAL

The Neutral Buoyancy Lab is a training facility located in Houston in the USA. It's a massive swimming pool containing 23.5 million litres of water and replica sections of the International Space Station.

Chapter 3

Training Disasters

Wednesday July 8th

I didn't eat any breakfast at all this morning, in case I had to go back in the pool. This turned out to be a pretty good move.

I had to report to a different training facility, this time on Jupiter Boulevard. An old man with grey hair and a jacket with the US flag sewn on the arm was waiting for me outside.

'Hey Ellie,' he said. 'I'm Pete. I hear you had a little mishap in the Neutral Buoyancy Lab yesterday.'

'Yeah,' I said. I felt my cheeks blushing and wondered if everyone in the Space Centre was talking about my humiliation. Was there a huge crowd watching it on monitors in mission control and giggling?

'Yeah,' I said. 'I may have barfed a little.'

53

Pete grinned. 'Everyone does that on the vomit comet,' he said. 'But it's the first I've heard of it in the pool. Do you get dizzy easily?'

'I guess so,' I said.

'Okay,' said Pete. 'Well there will be a lot more times in your training when you'll feel dizzy and want to puke. So you'll need to get used to it. There's something that might help.'

He led me down a corridor lined with pictures of astronauts from the days of the Apollo missions. I thought one of them was him, but the guy in the picture had thick brown hair so it was hard to tell.

We entered a room with what looked like an ancient torture device inside. It was a chair set in a black frame in the middle of three metal circles.

'This is the multi-axis trainer,' said Pete.
'It was designed to show what it feels like to go
into a spin when you come back into Earth's
atmosphere. But I also found it helped me
overcome my dizziness. I did a few minutes every
day and after a while I could handle any training
exercise they threw at me. It's a little like getting
your sea legs on a ship. Want to try it?'

'Sure,' I said. I got into the chair and fastened
the straps around my waist and shoulders.

'Okay,' he said. 'I'll give you a spin. Just tell
me when you want it to stop.'

He grabbed my seat and tipped it back. I was
amazed at how much strength he had for
such an old man. He pressed a button and
I was flipped head over heels, then side to
side and then diagonally. The speed of the
machine picked up and the room became a blur.

My stomach felt like it was a tiny rubber ball, bouncing around the inside of my body.

I tried to keep my eyes open, but it was no use. I found myself clamping them shut. A few minutes later, the sickening swirling got too much.

'Stop!' I shouted. 'I've had enough.'

'Er… I've already stopped the machine,' said Pete. 'I only kept it going for sixty seconds.' I opened my eyes. The room was still rotating around me, but Pete was telling the truth. It was my head that was spinning, not the room.

I undid my straps, stepped off the machine and staggered towards the exit. I didn't seem to get much nearer to it as I traced an arc across the floor.

'Good,' I said. 'Excellent bit of training there. That's enough for one day, right?'

Thursday July 9th

This morning I joined the others in the gym on Neptune Avenue. All trainees need to be in top physical shape, even ones who aren't really going to space like me.

By the time I got inside, the others were already hard at work on the treadmills, weights and exercise bikes. I didn't want to interrupt anyone so I sneaked onto the free treadmill next to the door and switched it on. It flung me off my feet and onto the floor behind.

I started doing press-ups, as though that's what I'd meant to do all along. I think I got away with it.

'You okay?' asked Emma, looking over from one of the weight machines.

'Sure,' I said. I was on my fifth press-up, and

it was already becoming a struggle, so I got up and strolled over to one of the exercise bikes.

I climbed on and tried to press my feet down, but the pedals wouldn't move. I looked at the display and saw it was set to the highest level. I switched onto the easiest one, hoping no one would notice. Now I could move the pedals really easily, but I made grunting sounds to make the others think I was having a tougher workout.

After a few minutes I was feeling confident and I strolled over to the benches. Most of them had huge barbells above them, but I spotted one with smaller weights that looked like I could lift them.

I lay down on the bench and gripped the metal pole above me. I pushed it out of its cradle and into the air. This was great. I was exercising with my fellow astronauts, getting into peak fitness to prepare for the challenges of space.

I felt my arms wobble. Before I could do anything, the weight crashed down onto my shoulders and pinned me to the bench.

I tried to push it up again, but I was stuck.

Dev and Li dashed over from the treadmills.

'I'm okay,' I said. 'I don't need help.'

But they could tell I did. Li pulled the barbell off my chest while Dev helped me to my feet.

'Sorry,' I said. 'Must have had a little muscle cramp there. You know how it is.'

Luckily everyone had red faces from exercising, so I didn't look too out of place as I blushed with shame.

I limped outside, feeling terrible for interrupting the proper astronauts. Three of them were actually going to Mars soon and I'd disrupted their workout with another silly accident. I was beginning to wonder if having me around was hindering rather than helping.

Friday July 10th

Martha Sanchez came by to interview me again today. She's going to do it every Friday afternoon and make it a regular feature on her show. They shot footage of me running on a treadmill and then talked to me in front of the Neutral Buoyancy Lab. I told her my training was going great, but I don't think it sounded convincing. She kept getting me to do extra takes, but with more energy.

It's funny. When I wasn't training to be an astronaut, I had no problem telling her that I was. Now I really am, I sound like I'm lying.

But the truth is this week was tough. Understanding the science lessons and lifting the weights seem equally impossible right now.

But next time Martha comes, I want to tell her things are going well and I want to mean it.

Saturday July 11ᵗʰ

I spent this morning running and this
afternoon reading, which surprised Mom and
Dad. I'm usually begging them to drive me
to the mall by three. Tonight, I recorded a
vlog about my training and put it on my new
channel. I already have a ton of subscribers, so
I need to make videos every night, no matter
how tired I am.

Sunday July 12th

Mom just told me to stop reading my science books and take some time off, which was a first. She's usually telling me to study more. But I have another lecture with Professor Conrad tomorrow and I really want to understand it this time. I'm ploughing through the books and waiting for the moment when it all clicks.

Monday July 13th

Okay, so I still didn't understand the lecture. But I held back from jumping in with any more Mars facts, so at least I didn't annoy anyone.

After the lecture I went to the gym and did half an hour on the treadmill. It was on the lowest setting, but I didn't fall off like a total idiot, which counts as a new personal best.

Then this afternoon I went back on the multi-axis trainer. I managed ten minutes this time, though they were spread out over a couple of hours. While I was recovering, I got Pete to tell me about the days of the Moon landings. He went to the Moon in 1971 on one of the Apollo missions.

He wasn't chosen for the first one, when Neil Armstrong and Buzz Aldrin walked on the Moon, but he got there before the Apollo program stopped.

He says he'll never forget the excitement when Neil Armstrong stepped onto the Moon and said, 'That's one small step for man, one giant leap for mankind'. Some people say he should have said 'a man' instead, which would make more sense. But others say GIVE HIM A BREAK, HE'S WALKING ON THE ACTUAL MOON AND ALL YOU CAN DO IS WHINE.

Two years later, Pete got his turn. I asked him what it was like to look down at our blue planet. I thought he'd say something deep about how it made him realise all of humankind is one or something. But he said he was too busy with his mission to think about anything like that. He had to check every piece of equipment over and over again, and he didn't get much sleep in the spacecraft, so the time flew by in a fog of overwork and exhaustion.

It was only later, when he had to talk to the media and take part in ticker-tape parades, that the importance of what he'd done sunk in. He said the Apollo missions brought everyone together, and for a while space travel was all everyone was talking about. Instead of a sports event or a TV show, the whole world was excited about a scientific achievement.

The Mars mission can bring that feeling back. And I can play my part in getting the public

on board. So even though I won't get to go to space, what I'm doing is totally worthwhile. I'm pretty inspired about it right now. I'd better record my next vlog before the feeling fades.

GET REAL

The USA's Apollo program ran from 1961 to 1972. It aimed to land humans on the Moon and get them safely back to Earth. That goal was achieved on July 20th 1969, when Apollo 11 became the first manned mission to reach the Moon. Neil Armstrong became the first person to walk on the lunar surface, followed shortly afterwards by Edwin 'Buzz' Aldrin.

This happened during the 'space race', when the USA and the Soviet Union competed to reach milestones in spaceflight. The Soviet Union was the first to send a human into space, but the USA won the race to the Moon.

Chapter 4
G - Force

Tuesday July 14ᵗʰ

Dad had to go up to see Bradley this morning,
but I wasn't allowed with him. I stayed down
in the lobby, worrying that they'd decided
my training wasn't working and I should be
kicked out.

But when Dad came down, he told me some
great news. It turns out I'm going to take to the
skies. I'm not actually going into space, but it's
pretty close.

To prepare for weightlessness, the trainee
astronauts are taken on a 'reduced-gravity
aircraft'. This is a plane that flies up and down
in steep curves. When you're at the top of one,
it feels like you're floating in space.

Bradley wants me to go along tomorrow and
make a video about it for my channel, but he
wanted to check Dad was okay about it before

asking me. It's a little more dangerous than the other training exercises I've done, though it's still not much of a risk compared to actually going to space.

Anyway, Dad was okay with it and he cleared it with Mom too, so I'm fine to go.

Bradley said it would be a tough experience and that the reduced-gravity aircraft is also known as the 'vomit comet'. So that's what Pete was talking about.

That doesn't sound good. If even swimming in the pool is enough to make me barf, I can't imagine the state I'll get in on that plane. But at least it sounds like everyone else will be doing it too this time.

GET REAL

Reduced-gravity aircraft give the sensation of weightlessness for a few seconds at a time. They trace a shape known as a 'parabola'. The pilot flies with the nose up at a 45-degree angle, lowers it to a flat position and then tilts it down 45 degrees. At the top of the curve, passengers fall at the same rate as the aircraft, so they feel like they're floating.

Wednesday July 15th

The good news is that I didn't barf on the vomit comet. And some of the others did. But apart from that, my little day trip didn't go too well.

We were all given special IASA jumpsuits to wear, and then taken to an airfield ten miles north of the Space Centre. We boarded a plane that had rows of seats at the back, like on a regular commercial airliner. But the front two thirds were empty, except for thick padding on the floor, walls and ceiling. I grabbed a seat and fixed my belt on.

We took off and waited while the plane climbed to the right height. Eventually our instructor Leah unbuckled her seatbelt and beckoned us into the padded area. We all had to choose a bit of the floor to lie on, and I picked one right in the middle.

Leah filmed us on a small camera as the plane climbed up and swooped down over and over again. At first we just rose from the floor a little. It was like when you drift out of your seat on a rollercoaster. But every time we went up we floated further and further. All I had to do was wave my arms and legs around and I'd be touching the ceiling.

'Don't make those swimming motions, Ellie,' yelled Leah. 'It's not safe for the people around you. Focus on keeping your arms and legs under control.'

'Okay,' I said. 'Sorry.'

We flew into our next curve and I drifted up. I found myself flinging my hand out to steady myself and it smacked right into Emma's face.

'Ow,' she said, rubbing her eye.

'Sorry!' I said.

'Like I said, try and control your arms,' shouted Leah.

On the next curve, I concentrated on keeping my hands at my side. Unfortunately, I forgot about my legs. I felt my right shoe connect with something and turned around to see Li clutching his neck and wincing.

'Sorry!' I shouted.

At the top of the next curve I felt my arms drifting, so I yanked them back before they could hit anyone. This time my elbow struck something and I felt a horrible crunch. I looked round to see Jack clutching his bleeding nose.

'Whoops!' I said. 'Hope that wasn't my fault.'

'It was,' he said.

It was at this point that the vomiting sounds started further down the plane. I hope they weren't brought on by the sight of blood.

Soon we were back in our seats and I was glancing around at all the injuries I'd caused. It's a good job I never had any real hopes of being picked for the Mars mission, as today would have ended them. The crew will have enough to worry about without the constant threat of me attacking them.

But hey, at least I got to experience weightlessness. And Leah agreed to send me all the footage she recorded, and I think I can turn it into a good vlog if I edit out all the parts where I got violent.

Thursday July 16ᵗʰ

They put me in a new torture device today. I reported to a training facility on Neptune Boulevard, in the east of the Space Centre. This one had something called a 'centrifuge' which turned out to be a huge spinning metal arm with a small capsule on the end.

The other astronauts stood against the back wall of a huge room, waiting in line to use the machine. An instructor with short black hair called Corey explained the machine to me as the others went in. He said it prepares you for the crazy pressure you get at high levels of acceleration.

He said there was a danger of 'grey-out' and 'G-LOC', but I was too hypnotised by the giant rotating arm to ask what they were.

The other trainees took their turns in the centrifuge and staggered out looking as green and confused as zombies.

Corey said there was a camera inside, and he agreed to give me the footage for my vlog. I've been getting hundreds of thousands of views for each video, so I forced myself to go in for the sake of my subscribers.

I climbed into the capsule and strapped myself in with trembling hands. Corey told me to shout 'down, down, down' if I wanted to quit. He said they'd be monitoring me on a video screen, and they'd stop it themselves if it looked like I was in trouble.

There was a large screen in front of me with numbers scrolling down it. I told myself it would be no different from playing Xbox, but I couldn't make myself believe it. Something told me it would be more like hitting myself in the head with an Xbox.

The machine started. As it sped up, I felt an amazing force, like giant hands pushing me into the chair. I gritted my teeth and told myself I'd get through it. The others had managed to cope with it and I didn't want to be the only one who cried out to make it stop.

I looked at the screen, but something was going wrong. It had gone black and white. This couldn't be good. If even the screen didn't work properly, what chance did the rest of the machine have? How did I know it wouldn't break apart and send me crashing through the wall? But the weird thing was that I wasn't nervous, just sleepy.

I felt something rising in my throat and then there was a bitter taste in my mouth and then on my lips.

I closed my eyes and when I opened them I was flying through space. I wondered if the machine had broken and sent me up through the roof. Why did they bother with all those huge rockets? I'd managed to break free of Earth's gravity without one.

I saw the Mars ship and wanted to stop but I just kept on spinning away, past Mars, past Jupiter, past Saturn.

I opened my eyes again and saw I was still in the training centre. The capsule was open and all the others were staring in at me.

Corey pulled me out and wiped the vomit off my face with a towel.

When my head stopped spinning, I asked him what had happened. Apparently, when I thought the screen had gone black and white

I was actually experiencing grey-out, and I couldn't see any colours. Some people even get a blackout, where they can't see anything at all, so at least that didn't happen.

Just after that, I'd gone into G-LOC, which I now know stands for 'G-force induced loss of consciousness'. This is when you faint because there's not enough blood going to your brain. Corey said it's pretty common to have weird dreams, so that explains why I thought I was spinning through space.

The whole thing was pretty horrible, but I can see why it's better to get used to it in training than be freaked out by it in space.

So now I've got to edit the footage from the capsule into a new vlog. I really don't come across well. First my skin gets pushed against my face so hard that I look about eighty.

Then vomit arcs out of my mouth and my eyes close. At least I'll never be mistaken for a beauty vlogger.

GET REAL

The centrifuge simulates the high forces of gravity astronauts can experience in rockets. They can lead to the loss of colour vision, due to a reduction of blood flow to the eyes. This is known as 'grey-out'.

As the force gets even higher, it stops blood getting to the brain and causes loss of consciousness, or G-LOC. This can be very dangerous if it happens to a pilot.

Friday July 17th

I had to do my weekly interview with Martha Sanchez today. This time I got myself psyched in advance and she didn't make me do any retakes. I told her it was all going better than ever, despite what happened this week. It was a lie. But I'm in the training program to get the public excited about the Mars mission, and that's more important than telling the truth.

Saturday July 18th

I was called in today to get measured for a space suit. At first I got my hopes up that I'm genuinely being considered for the mission, but Bradley Anderson made it very clear at the bottom of his email that it was in the rules of the training program that everyone had to get fitted for one.

I reported to a medical testing centre on Jupiter Boulevard and a team of two women and two men measured me over and over again. They did my legs, my waist, my head, my knees, my elbows and even my fingers.

They don't call them space suits anymore. They call them 'extravehicular mobility units'. And I can see why they need the fancy name. Each one is like a mini spaceship that costs millions of dollars.

We don't even get one each. They just have enough parts to make a suit for everyone, and they need to know which parts fit which trainee.

I got the feeling they were a little annoyed about going through the process when I'm only here as a publicity stunt. But I still kind of enjoyed it. I kept imagining myself strolling through the red dust of Mars in my suit, carrying rocks and dust back to the lab for testing.

It's not going to happen. I need to stop thinking about it.

4'7"

GET REAL

Space suits will have to be very skilfully designed to protect humans from the harsh conditions on Mars.

As well as being extremely cold, Mars is covered in red dust that could be harmful if you breathed it in. There are also very dangerous levels of radiation from solar flares. There is almost no oxygen, so you wouldn't be able to breathe without a space suit. And to make things even worse, the pressure on Mars is so low that your saliva and the water in your lungs would boil.

Chapter 5

Practice Makes Perfect

Sunday July 19th

Tried reading my tough science books again. Went for a run. Recorded a vlog. Too tired to write anything here.

Monday July 20th

I had another impossible science lecture this morning, followed by another session in the gym. By the time I arrived for my multi-axis training with Pete, I was out of energy. I just slumped forward on the seat next to it with my head in my hands.

'What's the matter?' he said. 'Don't feel like making yourself barf today?'

'No,' I said. 'I don't know. I'm just not sure why I'm putting myself through all this. I'm never going to Mars. All the others are cut out to be astronauts and I'm not. I'm not as fit as them and I don't know as much science. And every time I try and join in, it goes wrong. I'm only here to get the public onside anyway. So why am I taking part in all this training? I could just tell everyone I'm doing it instead.'

Pete pulled a seat over and sat down facing me.

'We all get this,' he said. 'Being an astronaut is tough.'

I sighed. 'I'm not an astronaut,' I said. 'I'm an imposter. I'm just here as a publicity stunt.'

'You might be more useful to us than you think,' he said. 'You've got one big advantage over the other trainees – you're different. When they were picking guys like me for the Apollo missions all those years ago, they went for competitive, athletic types. It made a lot of sense. They needed people who were fit, with a great survival instinct.'

He pointed up at a framed photo of the Apollo 11 crew on the wall behind him.

'When I look at the new astronauts, I can see they've gone for the same kind again,' he said. 'And maybe they're right. But what if they're not? What if we realise we want a different type of person altogether? All we'll have to choose from will be more of the same.'

I propped my head up.

'I know I'm different from them,' I said. 'But not in a good way. Why would they want someone who messes up all the time?'

'There's more to it than that,' said Pete. 'The Mars mission will be totally unlike the Moon ones. It will take a lot longer for one thing. We'll need someone who can stay positive in solitary confinement. I could be wrong, but I worry that the trainees we have will burn out too fast. They're used to a lot of conversation and a lot of time outdoors. Their life on the ship will be so unusual we've no way of judging how well they'll do. We might wish we had an alternative to throw into the mix.'

I leapt up from the chair.

'You mean that if I train really hard, you'll consider actually sending me to Mars?' I asked.

'It will never be up to me,' he said. 'But if I were you, I wouldn't count myself out.'

He stood up and dragged his chair back over to the wall.

Now I'm back in my bedroom and I keep running through our conversation. Was Pete really saying I had a chance at making it to

Mars? I don't know. But even if there's only a really small one, I need to be ready.

Tomorrow I'll get back in training. But this time I'm not doing it just to vlog about it or prepare for my next TV interview. I'm doing it so I can become one of the best astronauts and get selected for the mission.

Tuesday July 21ˢᵗ

Two hours in the gym today, followed by two hours looking at hard science books, followed by three minutes on the multi-axis trainer. I recorded a new vlog tonight and crashed into bed, exhausted. I really feel like I'm getting somewhere now.

Wednesday July 22nd

This morning we were called to the training centre on Mercury Boulevard to use the simulators. There's a replica of the crew module in the rocket that will take us off Earth. There's a replica of the cockpit of the Mars ship. There's a replica of the landing craft that will take us down to Mars. And there's a replica of the ascent vehicle that will take us up again when our experiments are done.

I waited for everyone else to go first, because I didn't want to steal time from someone who has more of a chance of using those things for real. But when I got my turn, I took it really seriously. I need to know every button on every vehicle in case I ever fly them on manual control.

The instructor Riley said I'd done well at the end of the session. That's the first time I've been good at anything since I started training.

Thursday July 23rd

We were back in the pool today, and this time
I didn't get sick at all. I managed to change
a panel on the outside of the rocket with
everyone watching.

I've really started to believe I could make
the Mars mission now. I know I only have a
tiny chance, but in my head I'm overtaking
the others and moving into one of the top
three spots.

Friday July 24th

I managed a stint in the centrifuge without
greying out or losing consciousness today. Corey
taught me a breathing method that let me stay
focused the whole time. It was still horrible, but
at least I got through it without dreaming I was
spinning up into space.

Monday August 10ᵗʰ

Still training. Still exercising. Still using the simulators every chance I get. Still vlogging. No time for this diary right now.

In two weeks, Bradley is going to choose the main crew and the backup crew for the Mars mission. I know it's unlikely I'll get picked. Really unlikely. But I want to make sure I've done all I can, just in case.

Monday August 24th

Bradley called us in to his office this morning to announce his selection. We lined against the walls as he leant back in his chair. He did a long speech about how everyone had performed beyond expectations and how difficult it was to choose and all that sort of thing. Then he looked down at his notes and reeled off the names of the backup crew, which were Dmitry, Hana and Matheus.

Even then, as those brilliant astronauts were being named as second best, I still thought I might get picked. That's how carried away I'd got.

Bradley read out the names of his chosen crew. They were Dev, Li and Emma.

It made sense. They're the best ones, and they deserve to be picked. Even with all the progress

I've made, I'm still way behind the others. It already seems weird that I thought I was in with a chance.

They're blasting off in three weeks. That's the time when the orbits of Mars and Earth put them closest to each other, so it's the best time to go.

Oh well. At least I was there for the moment the Mars crew were picked. And I'll be watching from the viewing platform along with all the other rejected trainees. I'll get to witness history. I just won't be part of it.

*Monday September 14*th
Dad shook me awake this morning and said we had to go straight in to see Bradley. I bolted out of bed. I was pretty sure I knew what it would be about.

The crew set off on Wednesday, and I'd been waiting for Bradley to call me and say he didn't need me anymore.

The public know who's been chosen for the mission, and they know it isn't me. So no need for any more vlogs or TV interviews and no reason for me to stay in the training program.

I pulled my clothes on and rushed to the car. Mom was in the passenger seat, so I had to get in the back.

I tapped her on the shoulder. 'Are we dropping you off somewhere on the way?'

'No, I'm coming in with you guys,' she said.

'Okay, that's weird,' I said. 'Any idea why?'

'No,' said Dad. 'It's what Bradley asked for.'

I guessed I must be in trouble if both my
parents had been asked in, but I couldn't work
out what I'd done. Were we being sued over
that time I hit everyone on the vomit comet?

Bradley was sitting behind his desk when we
got to his office. Pete was standing next to him
with his arms folded. They both looked pale,
and they had red eyes, like they hadn't slept.

Bradley gestured at the seats in front of us. I
took the one on the right, Dad sat in the middle,
and Mom went on the left.

  'As I'm sure you know, the Mars mission is
due to start the day after tomorrow,' he said.

This was the part where I was expecting him to
thank me for my help, then tell me there was
no need for me to come in anymore. But that
isn't what happened at all.

'What you probably don't know is that we've run into a very serious problem,' said Bradley. 'One of our crew members, Emma, has the flu and cannot travel. So you'd think we'd be looking to our backup crew. Except they all have the same illness. And so do all the other trainees. In fact, the only reason Dev and Li are fine is because they were in the simulators when it broke out yesterday, and we had the good sense to move them straight to quarantine. The fact is, we only have two fit crew members, and we need three.'

Bradley pointed to a framed diagram of the solar system on the wall to his right.

'So what do we do?' he asked. 'Mars and Earth won't be this close again for another two years. And our ship is waiting in orbit. The materials to build the lab and the ascent vehicle are already on Mars. They could become damaged if we wait two more years.'

He paused and stared at me. I must have looked pretty dopey because I was still trying to process everything. He was saying the mission might be cancelled because they didn't have three astronauts. But they did. They had me.

'Pete came to me late last night with an idea,' said Bradley. 'He said that you'd made brilliant progress over the last few weeks and...'

I leapt to my feet and shouted, 'I'll do it!'

Bradley held his hands up. 'Now let's not get ahead of ourselves. I'm just opening up a possibility...'

'Please let me go to Mars,' I said. My heart was hammering in my chest and I think I was even jumping up and down. 'I've done all the training. I'm just as good as any of the others.'

'Told you she'd want to do it,' whispered Pete.

'Okay, so we know how you feel,' said Bradley. He turned to Mom and Dad. 'But this is a decision for all of you. The mission will be incredibly dangerous and there's a chance your daughter won't make it back. I'd like to give you a few hours to think it over. If you think it's too much of a sacrifice, I'll understand.'

Mom and Dad were just staring at him in shock, like he'd slapped them with his laptop instead of delivering great news. They said nothing, so Bradley repeated everything pretty much word for word. Eventually Dad managed to tell him they'd like to think about it, and they staggered out.

Now they're in the lunch hall discussing it, while I wait out here. What's taking them so long? Of course I should be allowed to go.

Update

Mom and Dad emerged after three hours. They looked kind of upset, which made me panic because I thought it meant they were saying no. But guess what? They said yes!

Mars, here I come!

We went back up to tell Bradley and Pete. They tried not to show it, but I could tell they were overjoyed that the mission is going ahead.

I said I should go home and pack, but Bradley pointed out that everything I needed was on the ship. It's not like I'm going to want my beach

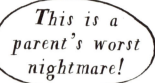

towel for temperatures of minus 81 degrees
Fahrenheit, anyway.

Then they drove me to a building on the east
of the Space Centre, close to where I'll be

taking off. I've been put in a room with a bed in the corner, and a bathroom at the back. People wearing face masks have been rushing in all day, running tests on me and getting me to sign things. I had the final fitting of my space suit, and all the different parts of it are laid out on a table on the other side of the room.

There's a camera in the helmet of the suit, so I'll be able to record stuff when we're on Mars. I'm also taking a handheld camera for the ship, so I can vlog from there too. It will take a long time to send the data back to Earth, but if I make the videos short and low-res enough, mission control should be able to get them and upload them to my YouTube channel.

Just two more sleeps on this planet. It sounds so weird when I put it like that.

Chapter 6

Blast off!

Tuesday September 15th

My final day on Earth. I was sent down to a
room on the bottom floor with a desk and a
large window that looked out on another room.
I took a seat, and Dev and Li came in and sat
next to me. They were wincing a little, and
I could tell they were nervous about taking
me along.

Sorry, guys. Too late to do anything about it now.

All day people appeared on the other side of the
glass and spoke to us through microphones.

First Bradley came in and took us through
our roles on the mission. Dev is going to be
commander, while Li will be flight engineer.
My role is 'second flight engineer' which makes
me officially the least important crew member.
But hey, I'm still going to Mars, so who cares?

This afternoon hundreds of reporters and camera operators squeezed into the space on the other side of the glass for our final interviews. They were all much more interested in me than Dev and Li, which must have been annoying for them.

The last people to appear behind the glass were our families, to say their final goodbyes. Dev and Li's parents managed to hold it together okay, but Mom and Dad broke down in tears, and I sort of did a little too.

I think the reality of what I'm about to do is finally hitting me. This is really, really risky. We need everything to go our way to survive.

I can't believe how much my hand is trembling as I write this. Goodbye Earth. I really hope we make it back.

Wednesday September 16th

This morning we put on our space suits and a guard came in to release us. He was wearing a suit that covered his whole body, like he was handling radioactive waste.

He drove us over to the launch pad. I was sitting in the back as we arrived and I stuck my head out to look at the huge rocket as it towered above us, supported by bright red scaffolding. The guard told me not to lean out of the window, like that was the most dangerous thing I was going to do today.

We got out and the guard led us into an elevator at the foot of the scaffolding. We got inside and he pressed a button to the left of the door. We rose up, and I could see the rocket speeding past through the elevator's metal frame. We passed the A, the S, the A and the I of the IASA logo on the side.

The guard opened the door for us at the top. He shook our hands one by one as we got out and walked down a red metal gangway. This was it. My last chance to turn back and announce it had all been a joke that got out of hand and I didn't really want to go to Mars. I forced my trembling legs on.

We squeezed through a small hatch and into the tiny spacecraft that would take us up to the Mars ship. We strapped ourselves into the crew module and waited.

There was a lot of waiting to do. Some guy from mission control talked us through all the checks they were making, and it went on and on. At least it stopped me being nervous. After a while, the only thing I felt was impatience.

It reminded me of the time we went to the Islands of Adventure theme park on Labor Day. I was really excited at first, but the queues took so long that the boredom was tougher to endure than any of the rollercoasters.

I tried to pass the time by telling Dev and Li what all the buttons on the control panel did. I thought my expertise might put them at ease, but they told me to shut up.

I joked that if mission control didn't hurry up, we'd miss Mars and Earth lining up and we'd have to wait another two years. They didn't react.

'T minus sixty seconds and counting,' said a voice from the control panel. Finally, we were ready.

Hearing the countdown made me imagine all

the people gathered on the viewing deck on the other side of the Space Centre. I remembered how badly I'd wanted to be on a rocket last time I was on it. Then I started to feel really proud that I'd made it. Things had happened so fast it still hadn't sunk in. But there I was, about to leave Earth. Even if something went really badly horribly wrong, it would be worth it.

I counted down from ten seconds, and I thought the others might join in, but they stayed silent.

'Lift off!' said ground control.

There was a loud metallic clank as the scaffolding was wrenched away, and I felt a mighty blast underneath us. The module shook crazily as we began to slowly rise. Numbers flashed across the screens, but we were rocking about so much I couldn't see them. Mission control were still talking to us through the control panel, telling us that everything was normal. That was easy for them to say. This wasn't my idea of a normal Wednesday.

We picked up speed, and it felt like I was being pushed down into my seat. The feeling got stronger as we rose up, and I got through it using the breathing exercises Corey had taught me for the centrifuge.

There was a loud bang underneath us and I felt my heart race.

I knew the rocket would fall apart in stages as we went up. I'd gone through it over and over again in the simulator. But in real life it was terrifying. It's just so different from any other mode of transport. It's not like the wheels of your car are meant to spin off on the freeway, or the back half of your plane is meant to rip off as you're eating your free bag of pretzels.

There was another mighty crash as the second stage fell away. It was so loud and jarring that I was sure something had gone wrong this time. But then mission control came through the speakers, telling us everything was going according to plan.

I focused on breathing in and out, in and out.

Another clang as the third stage fell away. Now the pressure was gone. Instead of being pushed down into my chair, I was rising up, held in only by the straps. This was it. We were out of Earth's gravity.

'Welcome to space,' said Brad. 'Congratulations on a successful take-off.'

'Yesss!' I shouted. I tried to hold my hand out for Dev to high five, but it floated up like I

was raising my arm in class. This whole zero
gravity thing was going to take a lot of getting
used to.

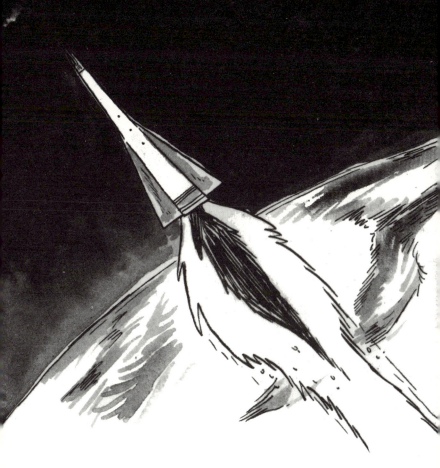

GET REAL

Rockets are designed to fall apart, so don't get too worried if the one you're travelling in breaks into bits. They use powerful engines to overcome Earth's gravity and carry smaller crafts into space. When each stage of a rocket has used up its fuel, it drops away until just the smallest craft remains.

Thursday September 17th

I'm writing this from my sleep pod on the Mars ship. We boarded in the early hours of this morning. Dev switched the controls to manual and lined up the nose of our spacecraft with the ship's docking port.

I've done it a million times in the simulator, so I had a lot of good advice to offer. But he said it

122

was distracting him and I should be quiet. It's just the same when I offer Dad driving advice.

Once we were safely docked, we made our way in. It's a lot bigger than the craft we left Earth in, but it's still a very tiny space to spend so long in.

The cockpit is at the front, followed by the crew's quarters, the toilet, the supply room and, right at the back of the ship, the nuclear reactor. There's also the gym, that huge wheel that revolves around the middle.

There are three sleep pods in the crew quarters. You don't need a bed when you're in zero gravity, as you can just sleep floating around. But you wouldn't want to drift into the cockpit and accidentally switch the ship to manual control, so you go into a small cupboard-sized room called a sleep pod, close the doors and zip yourself into a sleeping bag tied to the wall.

We also have computers inside our pods, where we can check messages from ground control. I'm going to use mine to send my vlogs back to Earth, which I know will max out our data. But I think they're important.

The only problem is that I type too hard for zero gravity. I keep pushing myself up to the top of my pod by bashing the kcys. I think

Zzzzzzzz   Zzzzzzzz   Zzzzzzzz

I developed the habit getting into arguments in the comments section of YouTube.

Dev and Li are busy in the cockpit, and they don't seem to want my help. They'd be surprised how much I know if they got me involved, but I guess it's up to them.

GET REAL

It would be just about possible to get humans to Mars using current engine technology. But the journey would be very slow, and it would be a one-way trip. This is because there wouldn't be enough room to store fuel for the return journey. Many scientists think new types of engines could be developed using nuclear power. Rockets would be faster, and you wouldn't have to leave your astronauts stranded forever.

Friday September 18th

I'm finally getting used to the space bathrooms. I tried to avoid them at first. I'm usually pretty good at that. Going on long journeys with Dad has trained me well. Whatever time we're travelling, he insists we'll get stuck in traffic if we stop, even if it's five in the morning and we're the only car around for miles. But a Mars mission brings a new meaning to the words 'long trip'. Not even I could hold out for months.

The space toilet is pretty much like a hoover, as there's an airflow in the funnel you pee in and the chamber you poop in that sucks it all away. It's probably the most important invention on the whole ship, as you really wouldn't want that stuff floating around the whole time.

Dev keeps offering me water when he floats through the crew quarters from the store room, and now I've stopped being scared of the toilet I can accept it every time.

GET REAL

Toilets are a serious and important part of spacecraft design. Yes they are. Stop laughing. Without gravity, poo and wee won't fall into the toilet like they do on Earth. As well as being disgusting, this can be dangerous, as they could get into the ship's electronics.

Saturday September 19ᵗʰ

Dev and Li still don't want my help. I guess we don't need to do too much anyway while the ship is on automatic control, but I'd be happy to take over while they sleep or use the gym. Not that they seem to be doing either of those too much at the moment. They just sit there in the cockpit, staring at the numbers on the monitor and murmuring to each other.

127

I've spent today recording vlogs in different parts of the ship. Even when I make them really short, it still takes ages to send all the data back. Dev complained that messages from ground control are taking a long time to come through, but I decided not to admit that my hilarious zero gravity videos might be to blame. He's already grouchy with me.

I really hope the viewers appreciate them. I'm reaching out over millions of miles. That's got to be better than yet another unboxing video.

Sunday September 20th

I still wasn't wanted in the cockpit today, so I hit the gym. That's the massive wheel that rotates around the middle of the ship. It's really strange at first. You float in, just like you would to any other part of the ship. But once you're there, the spinning makes you feel like you're back in Earth's gravity.

I can run, jog or just walk. You'd think it would make me feel dizzy to spend hours spinning round, but I actually feel less dizzy than in the other parts of the ship.

Now the novelty of zero gravity has worn off, the gym is my favourite place to hang out. I find it really peaceful, and I can jog for hours without getting tired. I have to get out of there whenever Dev or Li wants to use it, because they run much faster than me, but they don't go in as often as I thought they would.

GET REAL

Living without gravity can be very dangerous for the human body. It can reduce bone density, make muscles waste away and even cause loss of vision. Spaceships would need some sort of artificial gravity to keep passengers healthy on long trips. A good solution might be a rotating circular section.

Monday September 21st

Dev brought me another bag of water back from the store room today. As I was drinking it, I asked him how the ship could store so much water. He said that it couldn't. I was drinking recycled pee.

I was so disgusted I spat it out and it floated awkwardly between us.

He said it was fine because it had been through a purification system and it was better than most of the water people drink back on Earth. I apologised and gobbled up the floating blobs. I didn't want them to get into the computers and make them explode or something.

He led me into the store room and showed me the distilling machine, which has a huge spinning keg in the centre. He showed me how to use it, so now I can turn pee into drinking water without his help.

I'd like to record a vlog about it, but I'm worried it would gross out my fans. Instead of being that girl who went to Mars, I'll become that girl who went to Mars and drank pee. Those things stick.

GET REAL

Recycling urine will be vital on long space journeys. The international Space Station already uses a 'water recovery system' which uses artificial gravity to separate pure water from the contaminants in wee. The liquid that comes out is perfectly safe to drink. If you've operated the machine correctly, that is. If not, prepare yourself for the worst glass of lemonade you've ever tasted.

Tuesday September 22nd

Getting really bored of space food now. I eat freeze-dried fruit and dehydrated noodles, rice or spaghetti three times a day. They all taste the same, and when I complained to Li he said that food in space never tastes of anything, so it wouldn't make any difference if there was a fast-food joint on the ship. I know he's right, but I still wish there was. I could kill for some fries right now. And I've been in the gym so much I wouldn't even feel bad.

Anyway, they needed to keep the weight of this ship to a minimum, so there wasn't room for anything exciting. But I'm already planning the feast I'm going to bolt down when we get back to Earth. It will make me sicker than the centrifuge and vomit comet combined, but it will be so worth it.

GET REAL

Many astronauts have reported that food doesn't taste the same in space. This is because the lack of gravity affects the fluids in their bodies and blocks their sinuses. If you've ever eaten with a heavy cold, you'll know that even your favourite snack can be a disappointment.

Chapter 7

Stir Crazy in Space

Saturday October 3rd

I got a message through from Bradley Anderson
this morning. He says my vlogs are going down
really well. They've broken viewing records
and some of them have even been played on
news channels.

Now I feel the pressure to do a good job on the
next ones. I had to record today's video five
times before I was happy with it.

But it helps to pass the time and give me
something to focus on. It's not like I've got a
million other things to do.

Tuesday October 6th

Bradley asked if I could include Dev and Li in
the videos more. Hmm. I don't think they'd want
that. They've gone really quiet recently. I still
offer to help them from time to time, but they just

wave me away without saying anything. I'm not even sure they speak to each other much in the cockpit anymore. And Dev doesn't even offer me a refreshing pouch of recycled pee when he passes through the crew quarters.

Wednesday October 7th

I spoke too soon. Dev and Li weren't quiet at all today. And that was because they had a massive argument. It went on from the time I woke until the time I went to bed.

I had to stay in the gym to avoid it so now I'm really exhausted.

They should use the gym more, I think. And sleep more. And join in with my videos. I don't think sitting in that cockpit all the time staring at the monitors is doing them any good.

Tuesday October 13ᵗʰ

They're still feuding. I really hope they work it out, whatever it is.

We've still got weeks on this ship, then there's all our time on Mars, and the return journey. We all need to get along. At the moment it feels like a car journey after Mom and Dad have yelled at each other.

Friday October 16ᵗʰ

The good news is that Dev and Li have stopped arguing. The bad news is that they're no longer speaking to each other at all.

At least I get to sit in the cockpit now. When Dev's there, I sit with him and when Li's there, I sit with him. They both talk about how terrible the other one is and expect me to agree.

I don't really understand what made them fall
out, but I think Li sent a message directly to
ground control without checking it with Dev.
This annoyed Dev because he's more senior
than Li.

I thought these guys were meant to be the two
best astronauts in the world. They're acting like
a pair of first graders.

Sunday October 18th

Get this. I became mission commander today,
at least for a few minutes. I was sitting at the
controls with Dev and we were waiting for Li
to wake up and take over. But Dev became
convinced that Li was sleeping in extra late just
to annoy him. He said he wasn't going to let
him win, and he just floated away.

For a while they both just stayed in their sleep pods like sulky kids in their rooms. Which meant I was the boss.

It's really not a big deal, as everything is still on automatic. And I could take over on manual if I needed to, because I spent so long in the simulators.

A message came through from mission control checking everything was okay. I was going to mention Dev and Li's argument, but then I thought it might make everyone on Earth freak out. Also, I didn't want Dev and Li to find out and think I was snitching on them so I could become mission commander. We might be millions of miles away from the nearest schoolyard, but the no-snitching rule still applies.

Li woke up and joined me before long. He was really angry with Dev for abandoning his post, and he ranted about it for the rest of the day.

Wednesday October 21ˢᵗ

I couldn't get my new vlog right today. I tried to make it really positive, but every time I played it back it seemed fake. I think my worries about Dev and Li showed through. I'm really stressed about them now.

I need to end this. As soon as Dev wakes up, I'm going to call them both into the crew quarters and insist they make up. Our mission is more important than their stupid disagreement.

Thursday October 22ⁿᵈ

Okay, so I think that worked. I made Dev and Li apologise to each other and shake hands.

They're back at the controls together and I can't hear any arguing, so I'm hoping we can put it all behind us and get on with our trip.

Now that's done, I can finally record my next vlog. Those earthlings will get worried if I don't send something soon.

Sunday October 25th

No. Things are still not right. I went to check on Dev and Li today and they weren't speaking at all. They were just staring at the readings scrolling past on the monitor. I asked them if they'd had another argument, but they just grunted.

I told them to get some rest and they both floated away to their sleep pods, letting me take over. Maybe I really am mission commander now.

Monday October 26th

Dev and Li were both still asleep when I finished my shift this morning, so I had to shake them awake. Dev refused to move, and I had to unzip Li's sleeping bag and shove him all the way to the controls so I could get some rest.

Not that I got much sleep. Li had a sort of zombie look on his face, and I didn't trust him to cope if there was an emergency.

I soon gave up and floated back to the controls. Now I'm so tired I look as undead as them. I hate to think what aliens would make of humans if they met us right now.

Friday October 30th

This is getting crazy. I have to force Dev and Li to use the gym now, or they skip it altogether. They need to remember that they won't just get unfit if they don't exercise up here. Their bones and muscles will waste away and they'll die.

I have to take them out of their sleep pods and shove them over to the gym, then go back later and push them to the cockpit so I can get some rest.

How did things end up like this? They're meant to be the two best astronauts in the world, and I'm meant to be along for the ride. How come I'm in charge now?

Monday November 2nd

Mission control keep asking how things are. I keep saying they're fine. Sometimes I reply from the cockpit computer as Dev or Li.

I think I'm getting away with it. Maybe I should tell the truth. But then everyone on Earth will worry. This Mars thing was supposed to bring them all together, not stress them out.

Thursday November 5th

Okay, I think I need to say something to mission control. I'll try to sound casual and ask what they would do if their crew mates were acting a little weird. Hopefully I can get some good advice without freaking them out too much.

Friday November 6th

No, they freaked out. Bradley Anderson asked what exactly was happening with Dev and Li, and when I gave him a few more details, he flipped. This is what he messaged back:

I'm sorry to learn about the state of your crew members. We were aware that a trip to Mars would be a mental challenge as well as a physical one, and we tried to select astronauts on that basis.

It seems we have failed, and the pressures of the mission have taken their toll on Dev and Li.

Sadly, there is now no option but to abandon your mission. Our priority is to get our astronauts safely back home.

Mission control will send further instructions on how to set the course for the return trip.

In light of the circumstances,
I am appointing you mission commander.

I know Bradley is right. I can hardly take Dev and Li down to Mars and ask them to build a lab in their current state. But it sucks that I won't make it to Mars. We're so close now. We're just about to enter its orbit. Do we really have to blast straight out of it and go back home?

Maybe Bradley will let me come back on the next mission. But I don't think so. I don't think there will be a next mission for a long time. They'll have to wait for Earth and Mars to line up again. And in the meantime, the supplies and the ascent vehicle on Mars might get damaged. And they might have to rethink how they choose astronauts. Dev and Li were meant to be the best of the best but they've turned out to be totally wrong for this mission.

No, I think this was our big chance and we've blown it. They'll have to go back to the drawing board after this.

Saturday November 7th

We are now orbiting Mars. I thought the excitement might make Dev and Li snap out of it. But they didn't even want to leave their sleep pods. Dev zipped his sleeping bag so high that all I could see was his face and Li wouldn't stop playing solitaire on his computer. It's not even a good game.

I had to admit it. I was on my own and the mission was over. Mars was right beneath me, but it might as well have been millions of miles away.

It was time to set a course back to Earth.

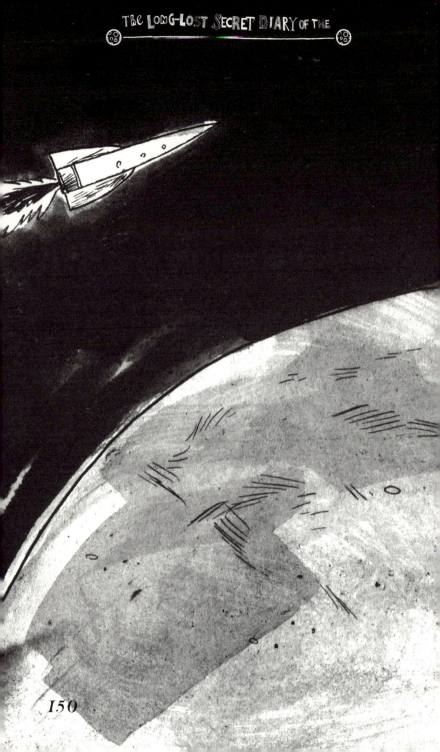

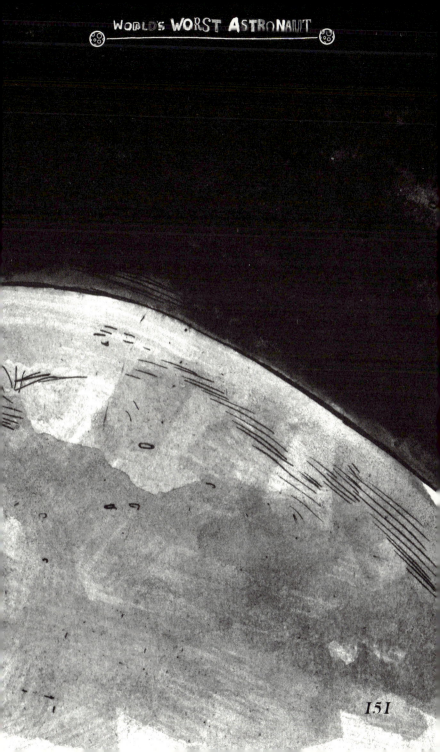

Sunday November 8th

We're still orbiting Mars. I keep getting messages from ground control, but I let them scroll by.

I can see the surface of Mars through the cockpit monitors. There are huge volcanoes, deep canyons and endless plains of red sand.

I've got no excuse to stay in orbit any longer. But it's Mars. It's the next step for the human race. And it's right beneath me. How can I turn back?

Monday November 9th

I just sent back a video announcing that we made it to Mars, but we can't go down to the surface due to technical problems.

They're not going to like it back on Earth. I bet everyone was looking forward to seeing footage of us on Mars.

But what can I do?

Tuesday November 10ᵗʰ

Ground control keep messaging me and telling me to come back. But I just can't.

When I was a kid we went to Mount Rushmore on the way to visit Aunt Julia and Uncle James. Except I stayed in the car because I felt sick after eating a big bag of sweets too fast. I should have tried harder to get out the car, but I didn't. Now if anyone asks me if I've been to Mount Rushmore, I have to explain that I sort of have and sort of haven't.

I can't help but feel like I'm making the same mistake again.

Every time we orbit Mars we pass our descent point. That's the place I'd need to set off from in the landing module to land near Gusev Crater, where the supplies and the ascent vehicle are waiting for us.

Obviously, the whole plan of building the lab and staying there for a while is out now. But perhaps I could still go down and come straight back up again.

Maybe I should ask ground control...

No, there's no point. They'll tell me not to. If I'm going to do it, I should just go for it.

Okay, I need to think about this. What are the disadvantages of going down to Mars? Well, I'd have to go on my own because there's no way Dev and Li can come. So if I injured myself there'd be no one to help get me back up here. I'd be marooned on Mars for the rest of my short life. Plus, if something goes wrong with the ship while I'm away, I don't trust them to cope with it.

And what are the advantages? Well, it would make a pretty cool vlog.

GET REAL

Once humans get to Mars, they'll want to stay for a while and carry out experiments. They'd also need a way of getting back up. It would be hard to land a big craft containing lots of supplies and an ascent vehicle, so it might be better to send these things ahead in smaller crafts.

Chapter 8

⊢⊣

The First Person on Mars

Thursday November 12th

I couldn't resist. This morning I stepped into
my space suit and climbed into the descent
module. I sat in the middle seat and strapped
myself in.

The monitor in front of me showed the
landscape spinning below and a readout of our
position. The descent point was coming up.

I figured I might as well go for it.

I pressed the button to start the undocking
sequence. This was it. There was no
turning back.

The whole sequence worked on automatic control,
but I had to check every detail on the screen.
There would be no ground control to talk me
through it this time. It was all up to me.

The descent module unhooked and drifted away. Then the engines kicked in. I was leaving the orbit of Mars and heading down to the surface.

I could see the heat shield burning up on the monitor, but the temperature inside the module stayed pretty much the same. It was hard to believe those intense flames were so close.

I pressed the button on my suit to activate the camera and mic and talked through what was happening. I told myself I'd edit it into a video back on the ship, but I was also doing it because it made everything seem less real and less terrifying.

The lander began to shake violently, and I hoped this meant I'd entered the atmosphere of Mars. I couldn't see the screen too well, but it looked as though my speed was dropping from thousands of miles an hour to hundreds of miles an hour as the atmosphere acted as a kind of brake.

There was a jolt above me, which I guessed was the inflatable device unfolding. I knew about this from the simulator. It was like a long row of balloons that worked as a parachute in the thin Mars atmosphere.

I realised I'd gone quiet. I tried to talk my subscribers through what was going on, but all that came out was a low moan. I needed to say something. These could be my last words.

I looked at the screen and saw I was just five miles away from the surface. That was insane. I was closer than my house is to the mall.

The outer shell of the module flew off and the rockets beneath me kicked in. This was it. I was approaching.

The monitor was showing the patch of ground I was closing in on. I let out a gasp. I could see the curve of a huge boulder right below.

I couldn't believe the ship had got me all
that way just to bash me onto a huge rock.
I hadn't been so let down by a computer since
my Dad's old laptop crashed and deleted my
history essay.

I switched the controls to manual and grabbed
the joysticks. A tilt to the right and a slight
thrust forward. That should do it. Much flatter
ground was below me now. I turned the craft
slightly back to the left to correct myself.

Then I felt it. Touchdown!

I slumped forward over the joysticks and waited
for my heartbeat to get back to something
like normal.

This was it. I was on Mars. It was time to get
out and explore.

I clambered out onto the rocky ground. I was in the middle of a wide plain flanked by mountains. I could see the small dots of the supply modules and the ascent vehicle in the far distance. It was hard to tell, but I guessed they were maybe two or three miles away.

The red dust was everywhere. It coated the rocks in front of me and hung in the air, creating a thick orange haze.

'So this is Mars,' I said into the suit's microphone. 'Pretty cool, right?'

I paused. This was the first time a human had ever been on Mars and I'd totally blown my chance to say something memorable.

There was nothing else for it. I clambered back into the landing capsule. I'd have to do another take.

164

I started recording again and climbed back out.

'Another small step for a human,' I said. 'And another giant leap for humankind.'

That was better. It was kind of a call back to the Neil Armstrong thing about 'mankind', but without being all about guys.

Now it was time for a stroll. The low gravity of Mars made me feel so light I found myself bouncing along. At this rate, it would be no problem to reach the ascent module. I might even have time to gather soil and rocks and all that other stuff we were meant to do in the lab.

The side of my boot hit a rock as I was coming down from a jump. This reminded me I needed to be careful. One tiny bit of damage to the suit and I'd be freezing and gasping for oxygen while my lungs boiled. I took a deep breath, and went on more carefully.

I tried to think of something to take my mind off worrying about my suit. Unfortunately, the only thing that worked was worrying about the ascent vehicle. It had been waiting there for over a year, gathering fuel from the atmosphere. It's been sending signals back to Earth telling us it's fine. But can you really trust what technology says? My phone tells me it has over 20% of battery left and a minute later it's dead.

I told myself to lighten up. This was the only time I'd ever get to spend on Mars and I was spoiling it with worrying.

I was getting closer to the ascent vehicle now. It was a tall rocket with four fuel tanks on

the sides. At least, I hoped they were fuel tanks. They could be totally empty tanks for all I knew.

There were ten bulky white supply modules scattered around the plain. If things had gone according to plan, we'd have unpacked two of them and built a lab from the stuff inside.

Here it is

The other eight contained enough food and oxygen to keep us alive for a month, and the equipment for our experiments.

I wondered if they'd get used by a future mission, or just stay unopened forever.

I spotted something out of the corner of my eye. Something not right. It was as if the landscape had shifted while I'd been walking, like a mountain that had been on the horizon had somehow moved closer. I whipped my head round to see.

It wasn't a mountain. There was a giant red cloud floating toward me. A dust storm.

I tried to run. Damaging my suit and boiling my insides were still dangers, but getting stuck in the storm was a bigger one.

I skipped forward with huge strides. It should have made me much faster, but it was hard to control my body in that weird gravity. I kept having to steady myself so I didn't fall over.

I hopped around the supply modules. The ascent vehicle was just a few feet away, but the wall of billowing orange cloud was gaining fast.

I reached the bottom of the ascent craft and launched myself up with a huge leap. I grabbed the ladder and hauled myself to the hatch on the top. Dust was swirling around me as I opened it. I ducked in and closed it, hoping I hadn't let enough in to harm the electronics.

I sat in the middle of the three seats of the crew capsule as the storm closed in.

I stayed there in the darkness for hours. The power switch for the control panel was right in front of me, but I didn't touch it. I wanted to save all the power until conditions were right for lift-off.

The storm went on all night. I fell asleep at one point, and dreamed I was arriving at school on the day of my history exam. It was actually quite a relief to wake up and discover I was alone on Mars in the middle of a dust storm.

Early this morning, the storm died down. It was time to find out if the power supply was working or if I'd been sitting in a useless tin can all night.

I reached forward with my trembling hands and pressed the power button. The monitors flickered on.

I breathed a sigh of relief. The electronics were fine. But the bigger question still hadn't been answered. Had the ship managed to harvest fuel? If it hadn't, I'd be stuck on Mars for the rest of my life. All three days of it.

I strapped myself in and set the controls for automatic lift-off. A countdown appeared on one of the monitors and there were loud clanks from the machinery below.

The countdown reached zero and the ship began to rumble. This was good.

I felt the vehicle rising up. Yesss! Tears of relief streamed down my face. The weak gravity of Mars disappeared and I felt myself rising in my seat. The launch stage fell away and I was soon back in orbit.

I switched the controls to manual and docked with the main ship. Now I'm back in the cockpit and it's

only just sinking in that I really walked on Mars.
I can understand what Pete said about the Moon
now. There's so much to think about while you're
on it that it doesn't feel real until afterwards.

Now I'm going to set us on a course back home,
just like I was told to a week ago. But first I'm
going to send the video of my Mars walk back to
Earth. I'll be so annoyed if this doesn't go viral.

GET REAL

*Getting astronauts back from the surface
will be one of the big challenges for a Mars
mission. An ascent vehicle loaded with fuel
would be very heavy, and difficult to land
in the first place.*

*One solution would be a craft that
harvests its own fuel from the atmosphere.
It could contain a chemical plant that
manufactures fuel over a period of months.*

Chapter 9

—

The
Journey Home

Wednesday January 6th

Hello again. We're finally back on Earth.

It's weird having gravity back. I just tried to pick up this diary by floating over to it. All I managed to do was fall out of bed with the sheets tangled round my legs.

OUF!

I'm back in the same room they put me in before we took off. Everyone who comes in to run a test on me is still wearing a mask, but this time it's for their protection rather than mine.

They think I might have brought back some sort of Mars zombie flu that will wipe out the human race or something. I can make them all run away just by pretending to sneeze. It's pretty funny.

I'll be out soon, but things aren't looking so great for Dev and Li. I forced them to exercise every day on the way home, but they're both very weak. They had to be pulled out of the landing capsule by medics.

We touched down ten miles north of here. We flew back to Earth in a giant ball of flame as

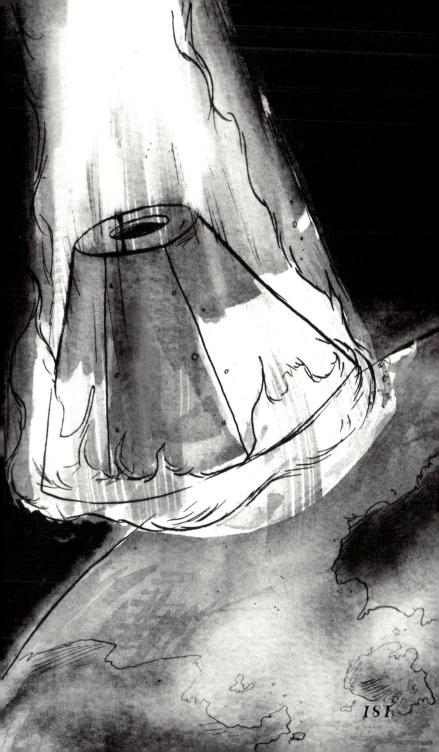

our heat shield burned up. Even though I'd gone through it in the Mars lander, it still made me really nervous.

Then gravity kicked in. My arms, my legs and my head felt heavy and I wondered how I ever took it for granted. Seriously, why don't we get tired of this constant feeling of weight?

The capsule's parachute opened and we were jerked up and down and side to side. I could hear the air ripping around us and it sounded crazily loud after all that time in space.

Eventually we settled into a smoother, slower fall. The rockets beneath gave out a final, short blast as we thudded to the ground.

And that was it. We were back on Earth. IASA helicopters swooped down around us.

A moment later, the hatch was flung aside and fresh air filled my nostrils for the first time in months.

'Food...' I managed. 'I want to taste proper food again. Do they deliver pizza out here?'

Friday January 8th

Mom and Dad were allowed in to see me today and they both gave me big hugs, even though the medical staff told them not to in case they got imaginary space disease. They said they were really proud of what I'd done and they read out a million messages from my relatives and friends. And from some people at school I hardly know but who are counting themselves as my best buddies now.

They said the interest from the media has been insane, and they've even been on the local news four times. I hope Mom didn't bring along any baby photos.

They warned me about the level of fame coming my way, and said they'd do their best to shield me from it if I wanted. I thought about it for a whole microsecond before telling them I didn't want to be shielded at all. I haven't had a proper conversation for months. Of course I want to be harassed by strangers.

Just before she left, Mom said she was a little upset I hadn't noticed her new hairstyle. Really? I've just been to actual Mars and she's annoyed I didn't notice her auburn tint? This whole planet and every hairstyle on it was just a blue dot a few days ago. That sort of thing changes your perspective.

I'm still very worried about Dev and Li. The medics think they can help them get fit again, but getting over the shock of all that time in space won't be so easy. It's really taken its toll on them.

Wednesday August 4th

I was called back into the Space Centre today. I've just finished a tour of twenty cities, talking about Mars in theatres and lecture halls and taking questions from audiences. And yes, they all asked how I peed in space.

I was actually kind of looking forward to a day off, but Bradley wanted to see me, so Dad drove me in.

When I got to his office I saw that Pete was standing behind him. It was great to see him again. He was the one who told me to keep going and who convinced Bradley to put me on the mission. I've got a lot to thank him for.

He was there to break some good news, which is that I'm going to be given the Presidential Medal of Freedom next year. He received it in 1971, and he told me all about going to the White House and picking it up.

Then Bradley announced that the budget has been approved for another Mars mission. They've already sent up the new ascent vehicle, to replace the one I used. For a moment, I got really stressed that he was going to ask me to go back.

It's not that I didn't enjoy Mars. It's just that there are other places I want to visit. I've never even been to Europe, and I hear the food there is much nicer than dried fruit and rice.

It wasn't what he was asking anyway. He just wants me to help choose the astronauts this time. He says he wants to find other people who can stay focused and positive like I did.

I told him I'll try. But I'm still not quite sure what I did.

Then Bradley called in a couple of surprise guests. Dev and Li marched in and thanked me for keeping them alive. They apologised for freaking out, and I said it was fine.

They're back to themselves again now, though I think their confidence has been hit. They've been winners all their lives, and I think they're a little ashamed that the isolation and pressure of space got to them.

After the meeting, I said goodbye to everyone and went off to find Dad, so we could get some food.

I had to do lots more autographs and selfies in the lunch hall, but I'm okay with that. I like being a Mars guru and I'll probably go on milking it for the rest of my life.

I'm sure better astronauts will make it to Mars one day. They'll build labs and carry out all the experiments I should have done. But whatever happens, I'll always be the first. And that feels pretty good.

The End

Mission to Mars

This diary is set a few years in the future. But how far away are we from sending humans to Mars in real life?

Not too far, but there will be a lot of problems to overcome.

The first is the simplest of all. Sending humans to Mars will be expensive. The cost will run into hundreds of billions of dollars, and it will be difficult to justify.

In the 1950s and 1960s, space exploration was driven by the rivalry between the United States of America and the Soviet Union. They both wanted to prove they were the most advanced nation on Earth. The world has changed since then, and these countries are no longer battling for space milestones.

But even if the money could be found, there would be many practical obstacles to overcome.

A spacecraft would have to be very large to carry all the supplies and equipment you'd need for a Mars trip. It would be hard to design a rocket powerful enough to launch the craft from Earth. But the ship could possibly be built in Earth's orbit, as in Ellie's story.

Even then, it would be difficult to fit in all the fuel you'd need for a Mars trip, and harder still if you wanted a return journey. And you probably would. It's pretty cold up there.

Some scientists have suggested building a new type of engine that runs on nuclear power, rather than chemical power, cutting out the need for huge fuel tanks.

But even with a nuclear engine, a Mars trip would take months. This would bring in a new set of problems. Spending a long time without gravity can cause bones and muscles to seriously weaken. This could be prevented with artificial gravity, such as the giant spinning wheel on Ellie's ship.

But it could also take a different type of toll on the astronauts. Being confined in a small space with no real-time connection to Earth would put a lot of pressure on them. In Ellie's diary, she finds that she can cope with this stress better than Dev and Li. Picking people who can cope with isolation and confinement will be important in any real Mars mission.

The astronauts will also be in danger from radiation from the Sun and cosmic rays. New materials will have to be developed to shield them from it.

If the explorers got as far as Mars without any disasters, they'd need to land safely.

A landing craft with a parachute wouldn't work in the atmosphere of Mars, so a new type would have to be created. It could feature things like expanding balloon-like objects, inflatable heat shields and powerful rockets.

Then there's the problem of leaving again. An ascent vehicle could be sent ahead to harvest fuel, so that it's ready to take off when the astronauts need it. In theory, all the ingredients needed to power the vehicle's engines could be found on Mars, but gathering them would be very complicated. And there will always be a danger that the vehicle gets damaged as it waits for the crew to arrive in the harsh environment.

Getting to Mars is the next big step for the human race, just as getting to the Moon was half a century ago. Scientists will always come up with brilliant solutions to the practical challenges. But whether they'll find the money to turn their ideas into reality remains to be seen.

Timeline

1957

Russia launches the first artificial Earth satellite, Sputnik 1. The Space Age begins. Later the same year, a Russian dog named Laika becomes the first animal to orbit the Earth.

1959

Russia gets the first spacecraft to the Moon. It's a probe called Luna 2, and it crashes into the surface at high speed.

1961

Russian cosmonaut Yuri Gagarin becomes the first man in space. He orbits the Earth in a craft called Vostok 1, returning under two hours later. President John F Kennedy seeks more funding for the space program so the

USA can catch up with Russia. The intense rivalry between the two countries became known as the 'space race'.

1962

President Kennedy declares 'we choose to go to the Moon this decade' to a huge crowd at an American Football stadium in Houston. The US space program now has a clear goal and deadline.

1963

Russian cosmonaut Valentina Tereshkova becomes the first woman in space. She was selected from hundreds of other candidates, partly because she was an expert skydiver.

Timeline

1964

NASA's probe Mariner 4 flies past Mars and takes the first close-up photographs of the planet's surface.

1968

The US Apollo program starts sending astronauts into space. The country is getting closer to achieving its goal of a manned Moon landing.

1969

The US space program strikes gold as the Apollo 11 mission makes it to the Moon. Neil Armstrong and Buzz Aldrin land the lunar module Eagle on July 20. Six hours later, Armstrong steps out onto the surface of the Moon, followed by Aldrin.

Timeline

1972

The final mission of the Apollo program is launched. Eugene Cernan becomes the last person to walk on the Moon.

1976

Viking 1 becomes the first spacecraft to land on Mars. It consists of an orbiter and lander that enter the orbit of Mars together. The lander then separates and goes down to the surface.

1997

NASA's Sojourner becomes the first robotic rover on Mars. Rovers are wheeled vehicles designed to explore the surface of planets. They collect dust and rocks and take photos.

Timeline

1998

The first segment of the International Space Station is launched. The first crew are sent up to stay on it two years later.

2012

Curiosity, a rover the size of a car, lands on Mars. It has been exploring ever since, looking for evidence that small life forms might once have existed on Mars.

Astronaut Hall of Fame

Edwin 'Buzz' Aldrin (Born 1930)

The lunar module pilot on the Apollo 11 mission, and the second person to walk on the Moon.

Neil Armstrong (1930-2012)

The commander of the Apollo 11 mission, and the first person to walk on the Moon. Before becoming an astronaut, he was an officer in the US navy.

Eugene Cernan (1934-2017)

American astronaut who was the commander of the Apollo 17 mission. As he was the last to go back to the lunar module, he holds the title of last person to have walked on the Moon. Let's hope his record is broken one day.

Astronaut Hall of Fame

Yuri Gagarin (1934-1968)

Russian cosmonaut who became the first human in space in 1961. He completed an orbit of the Earth in the spacecraft Vostok 1. He died just seven years later, in a jet crash.

Jim Lovell (Born 1928)

The commander of the Apollo 13 mission, which was aborted when an oxygen tank exploded on the way to the Moon. Lovell managed to return safely to Earth, along with crew members John Swigert and Fred Haise.

Sally Ride (1951-2012)

American astronaut who was the first American woman in space. She joined the

Astronaut Hall of Fame

crew of the space shuttle Challenger in 1983 and worked a robotic arm that put communications satellites in space.

Alan Shepherd (1923-1998)

Astronaut who became the first American in space in 1961 when he piloted a one-person capsule 116 miles above the Earth. In 1971 he commanded the Apollo 14 mission and became the fifth person to walk on the Moon.

Bill Shepherd (Born 1949)

The commander of the first long-stay crew on the International Space Station. He stayed there for 136 days from November 2000 to March 2001 along with Russian flight engineers Yuri Gidzenko and Sergei Krikalev.

Astronaut Hall of Fame

Valentina Tereshkova (Born 1937)

Russian cosmonaut who became the first woman in space when she orbited Earth for three days in the Vostok 6 spacecraft in 1963. She became a role model for girls who wanted to enter the fields of science and technology.

Helen Sharman (Born 1963)

Chemist who became the first British astronaut and the first woman to visit the Mir space station when she took part in a mission in 1991. Afterwards, she spent eight years giving public talks where she emphasised the importance of science.

Glossary

Atmosphere
The layers of gases surrounding a planet. Mars has a thin atmosphere that doesn't do a good job of keeping in heat.

Axis
The line a planet rotates around. The two ends of the axis are called poles, as with Earth's North Pole and South Pole.

Centrifuge
A machine that spins astronauts round to prepare them for fast acceleration in a spacecraft.

Cosmonaut
The Russian term for astronaut.

Extra-vehicular mobility units
A term for modern space suits, sometimes shortened to EMU. Astronauts wear them to do extra-vehicular activity, such as spacewalks, when they go outside the ship to fix something or carry out experiments.

G-LOC
A dangerous state in which astronauts lose consciousness because the blood is draining from their brain.

Gravity
The force that pulls objects towards

Glossary

each other. If you trip over on Earth, gravity makes you fall flat on your face in front of everyone. The gravity is lower on Mars, so you might be able to get away with it.

Grey-out
A sight problem astronauts can suffer. Colours drain from their view, because the blood flow to the eyes is reduced.

International Space Station
A science lab that orbits the Earth and houses astronauts from around the world. They get there in a Russian spacecraft called a Soyuz.

Mankind
This is a term used to refer collectively to the whole human race. However, some people now think the word sounds too masculine and old-fashioned to be used.

Multi-axis trainer
A machine that was used to spin astronauts up and down and side to side to prepare them for tumbling back into Earth's atmosphere.

NASA
The National Aeronautics and Space Administration, the space agency of the US government.

Glossary

In the future setting of Ellie's diary, it has been replaced by a worldwide version called the International Aeronautics and Space Administration, or IASA.

Neutral Buoyancy Lab
A massive swimming pool with a replica spacecraft in it, used to prepare astronauts for weightlessness.

Nuclear power
Energy produced by fission, or splitting the nuclei of atoms. Some scientists have suggested a nuclear engine could power a spacecraft to Mars.

Orbit
The path an object follows around a planet, star, moon or asteroid. An object in orbit is known as a 'satellite'.

Reduced gravity aircraft
A plane that simulates weightlessness by flying in steep curves.

Solar flare
An eruption of intense radiation from the surface of the Sun. This radiation would be very dangerous to astronauts travelling to Mars.

Weightlessness
The sensation of floating that astronauts get in space. It's also known as zero-gravity or microgravity.

THE LONG-LOST SECRET DIARY OF THE WORLD'S WORST

Shortlisted for the
Lancashire School Library Service
Fantastic Book Awards (FBA) 2017–18.

*'Although easy to read, the vocabulary is
great and the plot lines engaging – excellent
reads for developing readers.'*
Library Girl and Book Boy Blog

PB ISBN: 978-1-912233-19-9

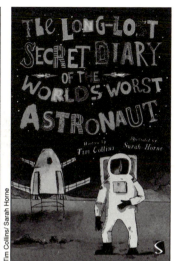

PB ISBN: 978-1-912233-20-5

PB ISBN: 978-1-912006-67-0

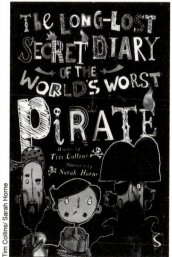

PB ISBN: 978-1-912006-66-3

A selected list of Scribo titles

The prices shown below are correct at the time of going to press. However, The Salariya Book Company reserves the right to show new retail prices on covers, which may differ from those previously advertised.

Gladiator School by Dan Scott

1	Blood Oath	978-1-908177-48-3	£6.99
2	Blood & Fire	978-1-908973-60-3	£6.99
3	Blood & Sand	978-1-909645-16-5	£6.99
4	Blood Vengeance	978-1-909645-62-2	£6.99
5	Blood & Thunder	978-1-910184-20-2	£6.99
6	Blood Justice	978-1-910184-43-1	£6.99

Iron Sky by Alex Woolf

1	Dread Eagle	978-1-909645-00-4	£9.99
2	Call of the Phoenix	978-1-910184-87-5	£6.99

Children of the Nile by Alain Surget

1	Cleopatra must be Saved!	978-1-907184-73-4	£5.99
2	Caesar, Who's he?	978-1-907184-74-1	£5.99
3	Prisoners in the Pyramid	978-1-909645-59-2	£5.99
4	Danger at the Circus!	978-1-909645-60-8	£5.99

Ballet School by Fiona Macdonald
1. Peter & The Wolf   978-1-911242-37-6   £6.99
2. Samira's Garden   978-1-912006-62-5   £6.99

Aldo Moon by Alex Woolf
1 Aldo Moon and the Ghost
   at Gravewood Hall   978-1-908177-84-1   £6.99

The Shakespeare Plot by Alex Woolf
1 Assassin's Code   978-1-911242-38-3   £9.99
2 The Dark Forest   978-1-912006-95-3   £9.99
3 The Powder Treason   978-1-912006-33-5   £9.99

Visit our website at:

www.salariya.com

All Scribo and Salariya Book Company titles can be
ordered from your local bookshop, or by post from:

The Salariya Book Co. Ltd,
25 Marlborough Place
Brighton
BN1 1UB